the TROUBLE *with* WENLOCKS

A Stanley Wells Mystery

JOEL STEWART

DOUBLEDAY

THE TROUBLE WITH WENLOCKS
A DOUBLEDAY BOOK 978 0 385 61007 0

Published in Great Britain by Doubleday,
an imprint of Random House Children's Books

This edition published 2007

1 3 5 7 9 10 8 6 4 2

Copyright © Joel Stewart, 2007

The right of Joel Stewart to be identified as the author and illustrator
of this work has been asserted in accordance with the Copyright, Designs
and Patents Act 1988.

Set in Cochin

The Random House Group Limited makes every effort to ensure that the papers used in
its books are made from trees that have been legally sourced from
well-managed and credibly certified forests. Our paper procurement policy
can be found at: www.randomhouse.co.uk/paper.htm

RANDOM HOUSE CHILDREN'S BOOKS

61–63 Uxbridge Road, London W5 5SA

www.kidsatrandomhouse.co.uk

Addresses for companies within The Random House Group Limited can be found at:
www.randomhouse.co.uk/offices.htm

THE RANDOM HOUSE GROUP Limited Reg. No. 954009
www.kidsatrandomhouse.co.uk

A CIP catalogue record for this book is available from the British Library.

Printed in the UK by CPI Mackays, Chatham, ME5 8TD

For Maija-Liisa
& Estella Mare

Stanley Wells walked between two lampposts on Zoffany Strand and thought to himself, I'm in a new universe now. It looks the same but it's different around the edges.

Then he thought about how he really hadn't entered a new universe, just walked between two lampposts, or that it could be a new universe but no doubt it would be exactly the same as this one. He was beginning to think about how one thought leads to another but how often they come round to where the first one started, when he stopped in front of the abandoned dance school and felt a very happy feeling.

The broken old building was boxy and black, with white and grey streaks from pigeon droppings. It wasn't the

usual sort of place to give a person a happy feeling and Stanley Wells wondered whether it had given it to him before. He couldn't be sure. His mother always told him not to stop on his way to the train though, so he stepped over a broken umbrella that lay flapping in the street like a demon's lost bow tie and laughed a small laugh as he carried on towards the station.

S tanley let the vibration of the train's wheels and engine mingle with his thoughts as he leaned his head against the window. In the three years since his parents started living apart Stanley had ridden inside more trains than he'd bothered to count. His dad's house was a long way away. Stanley mostly had to wait for holidays and then ride the train to see him, unless he appeared, travel wrinkled, at the weekend to take Stanley out for pizza. His dad seemed small and lost on these visits to his old home town, which is not a good look for a father, so Stanley preferred visits to the new town.

He rested his eyes on the faint morning moon because they hurt a little from trying to keep up with the blurring trees. He thought, rumblingly, about the chords he was learning for his ukulele; the pretty little four-stringed instrument had been a gift from his father and now rested in its case on Stanley's knees. Then he thought about how long and thin and hollow a train is, like riding inside a big tin snake, and about Katy Parcel, the tall red-haired girl from school.

This train was quite full but Stanley

had seen worse. It was good to ride the train today. Sometimes it could be a long, fidgety thing to have to do but today it seemed more of a warm, in-between-things kind of journey.

Stanley Wells may or may not have fallen asleep for a time – it is hard to tell with train journeys – but in any case the windows grew dark without him noticing. Occasional dim electric-silver flashes whisked past outside. Stanley's dad had once told him that one of the tunnels on this line was the longest in the whole of the country. Perhaps the train was in this tunnel now.

All at once the lamps in the carriage flickered and went out too, leaving only a dull glow from either end of the carriage and the pulsing passes of the tunnel lights. The other carriages were still lit. There was a scampering, scuffling noise, and another unusual noise that came from all around. It seemed to Stanley as though everyone else in the whole carriage was asleep – asleep and snoring. He could hear the snores even over the noise of the train engine. Then something cut out the light at the far end of the carriage for a moment and a cold draught caught Stanley Wells in the face.

A large, hazy, cream-white some-thing had begun to whisper back and forth along the length of the carriage aisle. Very fast, but with each pass travelling less far in either direction, like a giant pendulum coming to a halt. It moved faster and faster but travelled a shorter and shorter distance until it was nothing but a vibrating blur. It stopped right next to Stanley's seat.

Stanley fumbled for his ticket, dreamingly taking the cloth-draped ghost-like thing that was now towering

over him for a ticket inspector, although its blurriness had sharpened into something quite else.

For no obvious reason Stanley felt a sudden wave of sick-bellied sadness spread right through him as he held out his trembling ticket. This unexplainable new feeling, quite opposite to the one he had felt earlier, knocked clumsily at the inside of his chest as though it was trying to get out.

Then there was an ominous growling sound and the big, white not-really-a-ticket-inspector began to move again in a new way. It was the awkward dance of a scary, monstery thing that is suddenly very concerned with shaking off a biting dog.

'Grrrhhh,' and 'Eerrrgh,' said the sudden dog, and his teeth pulled a tear

in the cloth of the prancing monster, at which point it disappeared from the carriage as fast and whisperingly as it had come. As it swept away, a small round creature fell from the dog-toothed hole in its side and rolled to a stop in the aisle.

The dog grinned his top teeth at Stanley in a faintly worrying way.

'Nice hat,' said Stanley, very nervously. The dog went on grinning at him, paws up on the armrest of the seat next to Stanley's.

'May I introduce you to Morcambe Barnabus,' said a voice that came from the luggage gap behind Stanley's seat. Then a pair of long ears and a moon-white face appeared round the corner. 'I am Dr E. B. Moon, unraveller of ravelled things, untangler of the

tangled. Morcambe here is my faithful
and knowledgeable friend.' Dr Moon
tipped Morcambe's hat to Stanley with
a passing gesture as he leaped up into
the empty seat. He brushed the dust
from his suit with fast little flicks, and
then lit his pipe.

'It's no smoking on this train,' said
Stanley, impressed but still shaking.

His chest was still churning inside with inexplicable sadness.

'Ppff,' said Dr Moon, leaning into the aisle to pick up the little round creature. 'It's no smoking *anywhere* these days. But we shan't be on this train for much longer.' Dr Moon handed him the creature and Stanley finally felt the horrible sad feeling shiver and disappear as he touched it. The tiny, spotty beast had the most comforting weight of anything Stanley had ever held.

'Come on, both,' said Dr M. 'We do really have to get out of here.'

This new universe is not *exactly* the same as the old one, thought Stanley as he followed them out of the carriage.

As he clung to the train's roof, clutching his ukulele case with one hand, the wind riffling his collars and snapping the cloth painfully against his neck, Stanley wondered about this Dr Moon character and his plan for getting off the train. He wasn't quite as worried as you might expect. He could feel the comforting little creature in his pocket, pressed against his chest like

an extra heart. But it did cross his mind that all this was perhaps a worse idea than simply staying on a train with a scary thing. What, exactly, made Dr Moon any more trustworthy than that thing? He'd known him about as long, and now look what was happening. His wondering was torn out through his ears by the buffeting wind, bat-flapping into the dark tunnel behind him.

Now Stanley could see the end of the tunnel approaching over the carriages (the train seemed even more snake-like from up here). Each segment of train lit up in the daylight as it emerged. What had happened to

Dr Moon and Morcambe anyway? He couldn't hear anything but the noise of the engine, echoing all around from the tunnel walls, and he couldn't look behind him; it was dizzying enough just to cling on and look forwards.

At least the wind was beginning to die back a little as the train slowed to leave the tunnel. J229,891

HEEEEEEEEEEEEEEEEEE
EEEEOOOOOOOOOOORNK!

Stanley's stomach vibrated heavily as the train's horn blasted right under him. He might have been deafened if he hadn't been muffling it with his body.

Then, before he had time to begin wondering again in the bright light and calmer breeze, something tugged at his trouser leg and the train disappeared and reappeared several times sideways.

'Stanley – my name is Stanley Wells,' said Stanley Wells, answering Dr Moon. The two of them were sitting together on the grassy bank by the rail track. The morning moon was gone from above now but the sun shone whitely through thin gauzy clouds, pretending to be the moon instead.

'Well, Stanley Wells, I'm glad to meet you,' said Dr Moon, as though having your dog tug new friends from a moving train was a perfectly everyday thing to do.

Stanley didn't say anything in reply and there was an itchy silence. He took the little creature out from his coat pocket and cradled it in his hands. It really did make him feel better; the weight of it, and the shape, and its shiny black puddle-eyes.

'It's a strange day for feelings,' he said to himself.

'These are disagreeable creatures we are dealing with, these wenlocks,' said Dr Moon.

'Wenlocks? You must mean that thing on the train?' asked Stanley.

'Yes, Albert called them wenlocks—'

'There's more than one? And who is Albert?'

'My apologies, Stanley. I'll get to the point sooner or later. I am a little baffled – just generally, you see. One can't help but feel that these are things that oughtn't to be at all. Though all things have their place . . .' Dr Moon twisted his ears around themselves in a spiralling tower and then unknotted them again.

'As far as I can deduce, what they're out to do is steal feelings.' Dr Moon took the little creature from Stanley's cupped hands and Stanley felt a pull inside. He honestly didn't know why, but he trusted this pale, calm little person, and had done really from the moment he first saw him. But still, straight away Stanley wanted the little creature back from Dr Moon. He wanted the feeling of comfort it

had given him. All of a sudden he was remembering fully the awfulness of being thrown from the train, and the hideous feeling that came with the wenlock, and that his father would be waiting for him at the station, and . . . Stanley grew angry, but he caught himself before saying anything and simply snatched the creature back.

'And these little beasts are linked somehow. It's quite the puzzle,' said Dr Moon. His hands trailed after the creature as though he wanted it back too, but then they settled into the routine of re-lighting his pipe. 'And then there's the sleep-making — these wenlocks, they put people to sleep with a glance.'

'Not me,' said Stanley.

'You are a remarkably sturdy boy.'

29

Stanley didn't like being referred to as 'sturdy'. It was what his mother called him when she caught him worrying in the mirror.

'I think perhaps they weren't happy about your not sleeping,' continued Dr Moon.

'Nor about being savaged by your knowledgeable friend,' said Stanley, looking around for the dog.

'Precisely. And since that one was not the only wenlock on that train, you'll see why we had to make our exit as quickly as possible.'

'And as dangerously . . .' said Stanley. He carefully put the little beast back into his jacket pocket, where it belonged, and at that moment Morcambe came blustering through the bushes at the top of the grassy bank. A shopping-bag bundle swung from his jaws. He sat down beside Stanley and Dr Moon, grinned briefly and began to scramblingly unload the bundle. In seconds a very fine picnic was laid before them.

'That's right,' said Julian Wells. 'I called his mother this morning to check that he'd set off in time and everything was fine. Something must have happened to him on the way. It's only a short walk to the station – I suppose we shouldn't let him do it alone though; or we should let him have that phone he's been hassling for at least.'

'I'll get on to Constable Hocroft at

the local branch,' said Constable Pond. 'Take a seat for a moment.'

Julian Wells took one of the scratched plastic seats that lined the police station corridor and sat gladly. He hadn't been thinking straight all morning, not since Stanley's train had turned up with no Stanley. And there was something else: all the other children who'd got off when Stanley

should have – their oddly emotionless faces were haunting Julian. Their parents had all seemed so tired, yawning all over the place. Although that wasn't so strange for a Monday morning, all the passengers had been that way. But those blank-looking children had worried Julian somehow. He began to hum a snatch of music to himself while he watched Constable Pond make up a case file. It was an odd sort of tune and Julian wondered where he might have got it from.

'. . . and that was the moment I knew for certain that the leather canary was the key to the entire case,' said Dr Moon. 'I informed the constabulary of the necessary details and they took the whole gang of them, including Madame Gawp – the three-eyed, seven-fingered queen of pickpockets – into custody there and then.'

'How much further is it to Albert's boat? We've been following this canal path for ages,' said Stanley.

Dr Moon gestured forwards. Morcambe trundled ahead, happily muzzling along in the moss and weeds that skirted the walls at the edge of the path. Occasionally he turned, grinning, and his rump rasped against the rough red brickwork.

In the canal there were riverboats of all sorts, in all states of repair, huddled cosily together. Their paintwork was protected from the concrete bank by old rubber tyres and coils of fraying rope. The sluggish, tea-brown waterway was wide enough to allow the whitish sun to get through, despite the height of the buildings all around, and warm the glossy paintwork of the boats at least, if not the air.

Here the path cut under a bridge into a separate, musty, damp-smelling tunnel of its own and the canal turned a sharp corner. The boats on the other side of the tunnel were, mostly, more lavishly painted and better cared for than those that the trio had passed so far. One was actually turned all the way upside down and half sunk, but it sat as comfortably in the collection as the others. Somehow, with their colourful paintwork, steaming miniature chimneys and overflowing flowerpots, these boats were as homely and permanent as a row of terraced houses. Above them, an enormous weeping willow tree added to the secret village atmosphere.

On the roof of a boat with the words AYA LEE painted on its side a man was sitting alone under the leaves of the willow. Morcambe reached this boat and scrabbled through the collection of plant-pots and jumble that cluttered the slim deck. He shot up onto the top of the boat and claw-clickingly trampled across her roof to barrel into the side of the man, who lifted Morcambe's hat and affectionately ruffled his wiry head.

'Albert,' said Dr Moon from the bank, 'let me introduce Stanley Wells. Stanley Wells, this is Albert Lee. Albert and I were once at sea together, in the dim and distant.'

'Pleased to meet you, Stanley,' said Albert Lee as he climbed down onto the deck, expertly finding space for his feet amongst the mess. He helped Stanley to climb aboard and directed him up onto the roof. Dr Moon leaped nimbly across by himself and began to stalk around the boat with his hand at his chin, ponderingly.

'Make yourself comfortable, Stanley. The roof is the only clear spot, I'm afraid,' said Albert.

'It's a beautiful boat,' said Stanley.

'It was all we could afford at the time . . .' said Albert. 'How about a drink? Coffee? Tea? I know Dr M needs his coffee.'

Stanley chose coffee too, because he wasn't allowed to drink it at home, and Albert disappeared down into the cabin. Stanley watched Morcambe for a moment, wriggling across the roof of the *Aya Lee* on his back as if tickled by the fingery shadows of the willow.

Then he followed Albert.

Stanley stopped at the door. Dr Moon was inside, talking to Albert.

'He's a good, sturdy boy, Albert. I think he could be a great help to us.'

'Sturdy and unluckily adventurous, if he's got himself mixed up with the likes of you.'

Stanley interrupted them by knocking at the grubby porthole and letting himself in. Inside, the boat looked as if someone had dragged an angry pterodactyl through it by the beak. Albert had a lot of stuff in that long, narrow living space and none

of it was the right way up.

'Coffee's ready,' he said, picking up a tray and ushering Stanley out again. He suddenly seemed a little embarrassed or upset about all the incredible mess. Stanley followed him back onto the stripe-shadowed roof.

'Stanley, you must be very confused. Dr M knows more of this, since I set him on the case a few days ago, but . . .' Albert looked at Stanley with eyes that were circled by deep oyster-shell wrinkles. Stanley took a sip of his coffee and his own face wrinkled up at the taste. He wasn't sure he needed to be not allowed coffee. He might choose not to drink it whatever the rules.

'It's my daughter Umiko, Stanley. She's gone missing. She's all I have in this world apart from *Aya* here.' Albert patted the roof of his boat. 'I would have involved the police, but it's all so strange, I don't know what they'd make of it. I'm lucky to know Dr M and Morcambe here.'

'Did the wenlock things attack and take her? Was it them that made all the mess in the boat?' asked Stanley. At this Albert made a pained face and the oyster circles round his eyes crinkled up even more. Stanley quickly changed his question. 'You said she's all you have. Does her mum live somewhere else? My mum and dad live in different houses – different towns even.'

'I'm sorry to hear that,' said Albert.

'Oh, it's OK about the houses,' said Stanley, feeling just as clumsy about his new question. 'Lots of my friends have two houses, 'cept my two *are* a bit far apart . . . I'm supposed to be going to stay with my dad today . . .'

'Umiko's mother died, Stanley,' said Albert. 'She had cancer. Umiko was not much younger than you at the time. She isn't so much older now . . .'

Stanley put down his cup and moved his hand over his jacket pocket. He felt the creature in his pocket through the cloth. It was like a warm, round stone.

'Stanley, I'd like you to show Albert what you have in your pocket there, if you would,' said Dr Moon.

Stanley brought out the little

creature and cradled it in his hands. Albert didn't say anything.

'Morcambe took his teeth to a wenlock on the train, Albert. This was the result,' said Dr Moon.

'So you really did find wenlocks?' said Albert. 'Then it's just what I was afraid of, and just like she said: the wenlocks came to take the sorrows away.'

Stanley looked at Albert questioningly. Morcambe sneezed.

'That creature you have in your hands there, Stanley – that is what Umiko calls "a sorrow". It's a silly name, because they're more like the opposite, but she says it so seriously it'd break your heart if you weren't feeling better just from looking at the little thing. Don't ask me how, but my

Umiko can make them.'

Stanley stared at the little sorrow creature in his hands with curious amazement.

'Still, with the wenlocks I thought she was just playing around, making up stories – you know how little girls are: ever so dramatic, even those with less reason to be than Umiko. When she said they were coming to take the sorrows, I never guessed they were coming to take her away too.'

'The real wenlocks are just as in her drawing, the one that you gave me,' said Dr M. He pulled a folded sheet of sugar paper from his jacket pocket and handed it to Albert. Albert laid the drawing out in front of him and weighted it with the edge of his coffee cup. Stanley took another sip from his

own cup. Albert took his disgusted expression for confusion and shuffled a little closer to Stanley.

'The other week, when Umiko and I were walking by this old boarded-up building in Shroffold—'

'Do you mean the Eva Lückes School for Dance and Special Movement, on Zoffany Strand?' Stanley interrupted.

'That's exactly the place! How did

you guess?' said Albert.

'Well, I walked past there this morning and I had a very strange feeling.'

'Really? Because my Umiko got terribly upset when we passed it. I can't for the life of me think why. It was the evening of that same day when she started to make those little creatures. She kind of sewed them out of nowhere, more and more of them, over the next few days. And then finally she disappeared with the lot. I came back from work and found her gone, with no sign of the sorrows or any of this, except for the wenlock drawing she'd left on the table.'

'It's double strange about the Eva Lückes building,' said Stanley, 'because I felt very happy when I was there. It was weird, except that it's hard to think something is weird if you're being happy . . .'

'The feeling that you had on Zoffany Strand, Stanley, was it more like the one that you get from the sorrow creature there?' asked Dr Moon.

'It was the same kind of feeling, I think,' said Stanley. 'It's not easy to remember what a feeling is like

when it's gone. They sort of aren't real afterwards.'

Dr Moon spelled a series of 'O's in the air with the smoke from his pipe. 'I think you're on to something here, Stanley,' he said. 'And we should pay this place a visit as soon as possible.'

'But what about my dad? By now he'll be almost as worried as—' Stanley stopped himself from saying 'Albert'.

'Yes, yes,' said Dr M impatiently. He rubbed out the smoke rings in front of him with an irritated gesture. 'All in good time.'

'It's just a bust-up old building anyway. It's been empty for ages,' said Stanley. He got to his feet and walked to the edge of the boat roof. He looked out through the curtain of willow leaves at the higgledy-piggledy collection of boats. It was fun to be adventurous, but he was thinking perhaps he should be more worried about getting to his dad's than he was. He looked down at the sorrow creature in his hands and wondered if it was making him mostly quite enjoy all this rather than worry-worry about getting home. It was true though, what Dr M said: Stanley's dad would know he was OK soon enough.

When would poor Albert know that his daughter was OK?

Stanley turned round. 'I think you should have this,' he said, holding the sorrow creature out to Albert.

Albert took the creature from him. 'Thank you, Stanley,' he said. 'That's very thoughtful.'

'And we should make for the train at once,' said Dr Moon decisively.

At this, Stanley sat down heavily and shivered, his mood completely and

suddenly changed. He looked over at Albert, who was staring into the eyes of the sorrow creature. Then he looked down into his own lap and twisted his empty hands into a knot.

'I don't want to ride any more trains,' he said. 'Especially not with you.' Without the comfort of the sorrow creature, the very thought terrified Stanley. The big tin snake that appeared in his mind was not a good thing to ride inside. It was dizzyingly full of terrible creatures and seat after seat of unnaturally snoring passengers. It would hiss and thrum its snake-traily carriages through whistling tunnels, and there would be upside-downness, tumbling terror and heeeooorrrnking.

'It's OK, Stanley,' said Albert. 'I have a better idea anyway.'

Albert rummaged and scrabbled through piles of this and that on the deck at one end of the *Aya Lee*. Pot plants flew, hose pipes tangled, bicycle wheels bounced out onto the towpath and spun there like pennies. Finally, he emerged dressed as a black turtle, his circle-wrinkled eyes finishing the picture nicely.

'I made it myself,' he said. 'It's a

coracle. A simple and quite ancient kind of boat.' Albert laid the turtle-shell thing out on the grassy verge by the canal. On the inside it had a sort of wooden skeleton; the outside was black leather, or something. It was sticky looking and round. 'I have a paddle somewhere. Hold on.'

Stanley and Dr M looked at one another. Morcambe peered in at the edge of the coracle thing and it rocked when he pawed it. Albert reappeared, proudly brandishing a single, mouldy-looking oar.

'You paddle it like this,' he said to Dr M, swinging the oar round in a figure-of-eight pattern. 'You're an old seaman – you'll have it in no time.'

Dr M nodded and scratched the back of his head.

'You can get there by canal, you see. No problem. It's that way,' said Albert, waving vaguely down the river. 'Quicker than the train even, I reckon. I'd take you all myself, but the engine on the *Aya Lee* has never worked once.' Albert looked down at his shirt pocket where the sorrow creature nestled. 'Don't really know what I'll do with myself here, but I should stay around anyway, just in case . . .'

'Perhaps,' said Stanley, 'you could work on tidying up the wenlock mess, here on the boat?'

'Wenlock mess?' asked Albert, looking around. 'I suppose she could do with a bit of a once over . . . Here, let's get you launched anyway.'

Albert sighed as he watched Dr M slip the little round boat into the tunnel under the bridge and out of sight. The last thing he saw was Stanley Wells nervously gripping the edge of the coracle as it shifted unsteadily.

'She floats anyway, which is a bonus. I never did get round to testing the thing out,' he said, holding his hand to the warm weight in his chest pocket.

Then he picked up a long-handled broom from the deck and began to shake the fluff and cobwebs from its bristles.

Not long out of the other side of the tunnel Stanley Wells grew bored with being nervous of the bumpy little boat. He began to hassle Dr M for a go at paddling.

'It isn't easy, Stanley,' said Dr M, 'and we've no time to lose.'

'Maybe I'm brilliant at it! Maybe I'll get us there faster even,' said Stanley. 'Did you think of that?' He put his ukulele case under the bench and Dr Moon finally handed the oar over to him.

Stanley concentrated as hard as he could and copied the figure-of-eight movement that he'd seen Dr M use, but he wasn't brilliant. No matter what he did, the silly boat ended up travelling in wide circles and bumping into the sides of the canal, or spinning in smaller circles, making everyone dizzy. His efforts weren't helped by Morcambe, who was distracted by every moorhen and duck that paddled past, and by every squirrel hopping along the tree branches that now hung thickly above. Morcambe snorted and snuffled and made the beginning parts of barking sounds, shifting around in the tiny boat, throwing it this way and that.

'Stanley,' said Dr M carefully, 'do you think we are going to be getting there all that much faster this way?'

'Maybe not,' mumbled Stanley. And with secret relief he handed the paddle back. As Dr Moon took it

he also plucked a small tree branch from above, using a spare ear, and twirled it into the water with a plosh, and Morcambe followed it in enthusiastically with another, louder one.

'This boat wasn't even designed for two, let alone three,' said Dr M.

Above them the thin clouds parted a little and there was real warmth in the sunlight where it dappled through the trees. After the coracle had passed him, Morcambe stayed in the water, paddling behind quite merrily. Stanley settled back and trailed his fingers in the river, where small crowds of charcoal-grey fish tickled their tips. Then he sat upright, gripping the edge of the boat and looking intently ahead. Next he sat back again. It was hard; they were on an important mission, but this mode of travel was tremendously, irritatingly calm and couldn't be rushed. Stanley marvelled at the way Dr M controlled the coracle. His deft little movements now even seemed to balance Stanley's fidgeting, which was almost as bad as Morcambe's had been.

'That instrument that you carry, Stanley, can you play it?' asked Dr M.

'Yes,' said Stanley proudly. 'Well, a bit. I'm just learning.' He dried his fingers on his coat and fiddlingly undid the clasps of his ukulele case.

'My, what a beautiful colour!' said Dr M, looking back.

'Yes, I wanted a green one but we couldn't find one anywhere, so my dad helped me to paint it. We stained the wood properly and varnished and polished it. My dad is good at things like that . . .'

'Is he teaching you to play, too?'

'Well, he started, but we had a bit of an argument about it and then he said it was maybe better if I learned the beginning things on my own. I have a chart with chords on.' Stanley waved a crumpled, jam- and chocolate-stained sheet of paper at Dr M. 'I've learned nearly all of them,' he said, tucking the sheet back inside the case. 'It's hard to learn on your own, but I think Dad was right because I started to feel like I didn't want to play at all when someone told me what to do, and that isn't true – I really do want to be able to play.'

Stanley still wasn't very sure about doing it in front of people. When he played on his own, he often felt as though he was getting quite good, but it was different with other people around. Stanley had only strummed twice, however, when Morcambe joined in, howling along as he swam. The awful sound made Stanley feel better about his own noise. Moments later a mouthful of canal water went down Morcambe's throat and his howling turned to spluttering. After this the dog concentrated on chasing fish and paddling, but Stanley was happy by then to play without thinking. He'd never noticed before that time seemed different when he played. It was good: he imagined that he was playing the boat forwards.

Now and again, even as Morcambe ignored it as best he could, the music got inside him again and a scrap of howl bubbled out from the side of his mouth.

It began to seem as though dry land was floating by while the boat stayed still. There was the distant hum and clatter of a building site but it was pretty here, in patches. You couldn't tell how far from town a section of the canal was; the dusty, stony smell of cityish buildings with hard faces would be followed by stretches that smelled of honeysuckle and warm leaves where not one building was in sight.

Then for a while everything dropped away on either side and Stanley was astonished to watch a train pass beneath them, through a tunnel that ran right under the canal. The water didn't even tremble, and Stanley felt a little dizzy, the way a person can when things are stacked up the wrong way. He remembered being stacked the wrong way himself – perhaps it had been in that very tunnel – and his music wobbled a little.

There were several bicycles discarded in the water on the other side of the bridge. It looked funny when a person shot past on the towpath riding a dry one. Stanley was thinking that you could make up a song about sunken bicycles when he saw something that made him stop playing his ukulele altogether.

'Doctor,' he whispered. 'Over there!'

Dr M stopped paddling and watched with Stanley. Morcambe growled faintly from behind. On the bank, fluttering to a halt like the one on the train, was a wenlock! It seemed bigger and a little differently shaped than the other but there was no mistaking it.

Stopped in front of the wenlock on the towpath was a little boy, maybe six or seven years old. He was propped up on his bicycle by stabilizing wheels and steam was trickling from his tiny ears. Stanley shook his head in disbelief, but yes, steam, or something like it, was fuming out of the little boy's ears and rising like monster-horns to form a cloud above his head. The wenlock stood over him, and with its strange, soft, pom-pom eyes, looked down with a kind of stillness. The steamy cloud-shape boiled and tumbled over itself, and in the middle, like the wavy bits inside a jellyfish, things were happening.

It was like a dream made of dust and fluff, or a film projected onto something moving. It showed a little

dream boy, just like the real one below, shouting and waving on a shore as two distant people were swept away by towering waves. Stanley thought he could hear the dream boy calling, 'Mum! Dad!' but the real boy's lips were still. Out of the towering waves came great ugly fish with lantern eyes and slack, puppet flapping jaws. They swarmed around the boy on the beach until the whole cloud-shape was clogged up with night-fish.

Now the wenlock reached out its arms, and with movements very deft and fast for a creature with no hands to speak of, it wrapped the horror-cloud up in itself and tied it like a sack. Then, with movements even faster than before, too fast to follow, it made the little sack into a sorrow creature. Throwing back its head, the wenlock popped the sorrow creature into a suddenly gaping mouth.

All the while Stanley and Dr M were drifting by in the coracle. The canal current was slow here: they had time to watch all this and even another dream-cloud (a crowd of cruel faces) being taken from the boy on the path. Again, the cloud was squidged into the form of a sorrow creature and swiftly eaten like a grape. Then the wenlock whispered away down the path and was gone.

The boy opened his eyes, but they were blank and expressionless somehow. The expressionlessness worried Stanley in just the way that it had worried his father, watching those children climb down from the train that morning. Then the little boy began to pedal his bicycle, and to hum a monotonous tune. He didn't seem worried by what had just happened. He didn't seem worried at all.

Stanley was passing that monotonous tune through his mind, trying to remember it, when he began to notice a roaring sound and felt the coracle lurch.

'Hold on, Stanley,' shouted Dr M as they teetered on the edge of a tumbling slope of water. Stanley had just enough time to notice that there was a man

draped, asleep, over the bars of a canal lock beside them. He looked a lot like one of the parents who had been swept off by waves in the first of the bicycling boy's cloud-shapes. Perhaps the boy's father had been using the lock when the wenlock came along. The wenlock had sent him to sleep as he was shifting the great wooden arms that control the flow of water. Now Stanley and Dr M's vulnerable little craft was being pulled into the weir beside the lock extra fast because the lock was over-filled.

Stanley dropped his ukulele into its open case in the bottom of the boat and grasped the wooden bench with both hands. Their boat began to spin around madly at the tip of the weir. Stanley caught sight of Morcambe soppingly clambering out onto the bank as the world flashed round. He thought he could still hear the blank-faced little boy humming too, but that couldn't be right because, looking ahead again, he found that he could see Dr M's mouth moving but couldn't make out any shouting over the noise of the water. The boat went on spinning like a fairground ride. Then Stanley suddenly felt all his thoughts trail out above his head as the coracle plummeted down the cascade of rushing water.

With a bump and a tip, they hit the walls at the narrow end of the weir, where the water turned and funnelled out fast into the next section of canal. For a moment it seemed as though they would stay stuck between the slimy, algae-covered walls. Stanley caught Dr M's eye and wasn't reassured. Then, as the water built up behind them, the skeleton ribs of the coracle flexed and they shot through and over the edge of a wall of foaming water. It seemed, to wide-eyed, terrified Stanley, a terrible height; a proper waterfall. For a few seconds the coracle was an upended parachute, falling through thin air

exactly as fast as parachutes don't. Then it skimmed and bounced across the surface of the water below and finally came to a stop, mounted on a patch of sticks and rubbish.

A family of moorhens immediately surrounded the boat, complaining and squawking at it with dragon-like ferociousness. Stanley Wells peered shakily over the edge of the boat at the angry birds. Dr Moon stood up and straightened his suit.

From their noisy perch, Stanley and Dr M saw Morcambe high above them, looking down. He wagged his tail wildly and then ran away, disappearing from view over the edge of the lock. Stanley watched the towpath, expecting Morcambe to come running round to them that way. But when he heard an excited yelp he turned just in time to see him shoot delightedly over the waterfall at the same spot that their boat had, teeth flashing in the foam.

'He's never been one for being left out,' said Dr M, lighting his pipe as Morcambe paddled over to them, snuffling with wet excitement.

Even without a comforting creature in his coat pocket, Stanley was getting used to being tossed through the air, but still he concentrated hard on the scene that they had witnessed, perhaps as much to forget about skimming boats and fast plummeting as to be solving mysteries.

'What we saw above that boy's head, that wasn't real, was it? Hadn't really happened?' asked Stanley, ruffling his own hair as if to make sure he'd re-packed his thoughts. Dr M had untangled the coracle from its perch, leaving the poor moorhens to tidy up their home, and the boat was floating calmly downstream again. 'I mean, his dad wasn't really swept off by giant waves because I saw him sleeping on the lock.'

'What we saw there,' said Dr M, 'was an inside thing. Something, a feeling or a fear, that belonged to that little boy. The wenlock pulled it out and took it away.'

'That's sort of what I thought,' said Stanley. 'You'd think it might be good to get rid of a nasty "inside thing" like that, but he didn't look right afterwards.'

'No, Stanley, he didn't. Those kinds of things are complicated and hard. Sometimes they're foolish and silly, too, but they aren't for stealing.'

'Should we have stayed with him, do you think?'

'I really don't think there's a lot we could do for him that way, and very likely he isn't the only person this has happened to; the wenlocks seem to be getting about a bit,' said Dr M. 'Best to stick to the plan. His father should wake soon and they'll have each other at least.'

Stanley picked up his ukulele from the open case and looked it over carefully. He polished one or two droplets of water away with his coat-sleeve. No damage done.

Nobody said anything much more for a while. Stanley thought about Umiko Lee. Her mother wasn't going to wake soon like the man on the lock. It was a sad thought, so big that he could hardly grasp it. Stanley tried again to remember that humming tune instead. It was funny – he felt like it was there inside him somewhere, but when he got close to remembering it slipped out of reach like something floating on water.

The sun was lower in the sky now and cast a rich, tawny-grey light onto the buildings, which were gathering in tighter and tighter crowds beside the canal.

'That's the place, there,' said Stanley suddenly. 'I didn't even recognize the town, looking at it from here on the water, but that over there is the place we're heading for. I know because of the wind thingy.'

Dr Moon followed Stanley's pointing finger and saw, high up between the roofwork and jostling town towers, a weathervane in the shape of a dancing girl.

'Appropriate enough. You're sure though?' he said.

'Oh yes, you can actually see her

from my bedroom window at my mum's house. I've got a high-up bed and you can see out over the town. Sometimes the moon stops behind her: I drew a picture of it once.'

Dr M nudged the coracle in to the side of the canal and hopped out. He held out a tiny hand for Stanley. Morcambe scrabbled out of the water some way behind. Running over, he greeted Stanley and Dr M with an enthusiastic shower of fur-flung canal water. Dr M sighed a long-suffering sigh and once again re-lit his splash-extinguished pipe.

'Here, help me pull in the coracle, Stanley,' he said, and they lifted the boat out of the water and tipped it onto its edge. It didn't weigh all that much and Dr M carried it off on his back, looking like a big woodlouse with one paddly feeler. He propped the boat in a shadowy corner under a nearby bridge.

They took a narrow, upward-winding path from the canal. This was why Stanley didn't recognize his home town from this angle; it was one of those paths that his mother said he shouldn't go down. The walls were high on either side and leaned inwards, threatening a flattening. Small doors appeared every now and again in the walls, thoroughly closed and very old looking, but new at the same time, with fresh graffiti and scrape-marks. Not the best part of town. It smelled bad here too, though damp Morcambe in an enclosed space was adding to that.

Morcambe wagged and Stanley

breathed a sigh of relief as they stepped
out from the gloomy path onto a wide
street. Looking up, Stanley spotted
the dancing girl weathervane again,
and there was music and the happy
thrumming of voices coming from a
short way down the street. Stanley, Dr
M and Morcambe peered
round the corner.

A street party was in
full swing. Adults were
dancing and chatting,
pouring drinks and
munching cakes from
tables scattered out
over the road. There
were children around
too, but they stood
apart from one another;
saying and doing little

except humming. They all hummed the same tune to themselves, a constant drone beneath the happy sounds of the party.

'This is Zoffany Strand. They're right in front of the school. I think the happy feeling got to them too,' whispered Stanley.

'But not the children. Something else has got to them,' whispered Dr M back.

'What does Umiko look like, Doctor?' asked Stanley.

'Well, I've never met Umiko, but her mother was Japanese and I don't see anyone who looks at all like that here. We'd better see if there is a back way into your happy old building.'

There was a back door to the big black building and it opened with an

easy creak. The chain-lock that had
held it was already broken. Inside the
shadowy corridor, Stanley looked down
and saw Morcambe's grin flashing
in the dim. He knew the feeling. It
was fantastic in here. All the brilliant
rubbish and old bottles that tramps
had left, and the marvellous monsters

that might be waiting at the top of the stairs ahead, or lurking in the shadows beneath. Stanley felt wonderful. His chest was filled with a warm syrupy feeling as the three of them climbed the twisting staircase.

Umiko Lee was dancing. Her hair fanned out in a circle and her fingers trailed gracefully. She crossed the wide room with fast-tipping toes and didn't step on a single creature. She reached the tall mirrored wall and flipped over to stand on her head, her hair folded down like an umbrella blown inside-out. She puffed stray strands from her eyes and saw a thousand

sorrow creatures, tumbled out across the ceiling, and a line of Umikos hanging there, smudging endless mirrors with their heels. Great silver moons stuck up on stalks from the floor. The mirrors reflected everything over and over, almost infinitely, on two sides of the room.

Then a thousand dogs in a thousand hats strolled across the ceiling into the

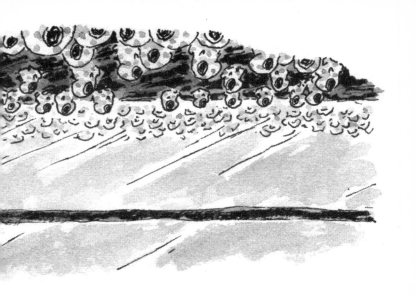

main hall of the Eva Lückes School for Dance and Special Movement. Umiko rolled over and turned the ceiling back into the floor. Morcambe grinned at her and wagged. She grinned back.

'Hallo, dog,' she said cheerfully. 'I like your hat.'

Stanley peeked into the wide room after Morcambe and gasped. Turning to Dr M behind him in the dark, he whispered, 'We've done it! I think we've found her. I think we've definitely found her.'

Dr M picked his way past first Stanley and then Morcambe, over the spotty sea of creatures on the floor, to Umiko.

'Dear Umiko, I am Dr E. B. Moon. I have known your father for longer than I can recall.' He held out his hand for her to shake.

'Oh, you're a wonder, aren't you?' she said, taking the hand. 'I wonder what kind of a wonder you are?' She dragged Dr M back across the room, knelt in front of Morcambe and began to pet him with her free hand. 'And who else have you brought?' she said, looking up at Stanley, who was standing shyly (but feeling very fine) by the door. 'I didn't want visitors here, really. But this is all very exciting.'

'I'm very sorry about your mum,' blurted Stanley, immediately feeling unsure and stupid for saying it. It was too weird to feel this stupid and this good at the same time. All these happy-making sorrow creatures in the room made him dizzy – there would have been enough for that even if there hadn't been the multiplying mirrors effect. He wondered if that might be why Umiko seemed a little odd, too. But now he could see for certain that the creatures here were the reason for the strange feeling he'd had as he walked past in the morning. The good feeling radiated out from them like the rays on a drawing of the sun. And all those partying grown-ups outside were feeling it too.

'This is Stanley Wells,' said Dr M. 'He helped me to find this place and we're both helping your father. Albert is very worried about you, you know.'

Umiko's expression flickered, just slightly. 'Oh, but he likes *me* to be helpful, and that's what I'm being.'

'He thinks you've been terribly kidnapped.'

'Oh, dear. He doesn't know anything about all this, really,' said Umiko. 'It was a secret. Always meant to be a surprise. Me and Mum had it all planned. We used to come here together, when Dad was at work.' She let go of Dr M's hand and danced out into the centre of the room, where she twirled and pranced about amongst the spotty sea. 'And we danced and danced.'

Umiko kicked up dust and twirled faster and faster and faster; then she fell over.

She picked a sorrow creature up from beside her and balanced it between her drawn-up knees. She smiled at the little beast. A dusty shaft of light, cast in from one of the many gaps between the boarded windows, lit her face, and Stanley saw a tear roll down her cheek. 'We were just learning, taking lessons. It was a good school. Mum was rubbish, and Eva wasn't the best teacher, but we were getting better. We were going to surprise Dad with it one day, when we got brilliant.

'Then . . . then she got ill and we stopped

116

coming. I couldn't ever tell Dad about it.' Umiko picked up another creature from the floor and arranged them, one on each knee, looking at one another. 'I thought about this place sometimes, but I sort of began to forget after a while . . . it was almost like I was being sad about forgetting, instead of about what I remembered. Then me and Dad walked past this place the other week, all closed up, and I suddenly couldn't do any more forgetting.'

'Your father said that was the day that you began to make these creatures. Where did you learn to do that?' asked Dr M.

'I don't know, I just kind of knew it. Mum wasn't a great dancer – yet – but she was always good at making things and so I made things too, because I was thinking of her. I sewed out the sad feeling, and when it looked back at me it made me happy. With each one I made I felt a little lighter.'

'It takes a lot of care to make such a beautiful thing, and they do seem to turn the sadness around somehow,' said Dr M. 'But you knew that the wenlock creatures were coming to kidnap you?'

'Kidnap . . .' said Umiko distantly.

'It is my deduction,' continued Dr M, ignoring her, 'that these wonderful things that you've made' – he gestured around at the sorrows – 'have summoned up some kind of ancient force, a force that breathes in

118

sadness, worry and fears: feelings that are always around somewhere where people are – or any creatures, for that matter.'

Umiko cocked her head on one side, and looked puzzled.

'But you've given a more solid shape to these feelings with your sorrow creatures, and this ancient force has taken a solid shape of its own to feed off them in turn,' concluded Dr M.

'I don't understand, but you're talking about my wenlocks, aren't you?' said Umiko.

'*Your* wenlocks?' said Dr M.

'I don't know about any ancient forces or whatever. I made the sorrow creatures because they helped me to feel better, and then I made a new thing – three new things actually, so far, and I've almost enough here for another. I made them, and named them myself, and now my wenlocks are out where they can help other people with sad feelings and frights and worries. They can just take them right away.'

'Oh dear, yes, I see. I was getting carried away myself. It's simpler than I thought,' said Dr M, tapping his pipe. 'It's strange though, isn't it, that this great group of creatures here can give out such a good feeling, even though they are made of things quite the opposite, but one wenlock is so filled up with sadness – I think I am right here at least – that a person nearby can do nothing but fall asleep to escape. Do they not send you to sleep?'

'No . . . Well, after I sent them out the first time they did make me feel a little bit different, and the second time a bit more . . . It *was* a sleepy feeling, now that I think about it.'

'Interesting . . .' said Dr M.

'I only made them; it doesn't mean that I understand them,' said Umiko, taking the two creatures off her knees and slapping her hands there instead, encouraging Morcambe to run to her.

'Yes, I'm afraid that's very true,' said Dr M.

'But I know that everyone has fears and worries and sad things,' said Umiko, 'and now I know how to make them go away.' She raised her hands above Morcambe and made herself very still. Morcambe stopped wiggling for the first time since he'd entered the building. His fur seemed to straighten and his ears lifted a little where they

joined his head.

Umiko's hands fluttered in the air like hummingbirds, and then she had Morcambe's sorrow creature in them. Her movements were so fast – faster even than the wenlock's – that it was impossible to see how it was done. She put the creature down. Stanley tried to keep track of it, but lumpy though it was, it was quickly lost amongst the others.

Morcambe sat very still for a moment; then he got up and blankly walked away. As he walked, a droning tune came from his throat. Stanley thought he saw all the sorrow creatures in the room shift a little when he made that noise. Umiko watched

Morcambe with a look of concern.

'The feeling would be too stiff and stuck inside a grown-up person – been around too long maybe – to get the feeling out, I mean. It's easy with children or animals, but I don't know how to help the poor grown-ups,' she said.

'But you haven't ever actually taken them from someone else before, have you? Not in person,' said Dr M.

'Well, no, not exactly. I sent my wenlocks out for that. How did you know that?'

'I can see the look in your eyes. Morcambe's not quite right now, is he?'

'I . . . He . . . There is something funny . . .'

Umiko stood up and began dance around the room again. Dr M went over to one of the tall, darkened windows. He pulled at the edge of the board that covered it and let in a little more dusty light.

'Come and look, Umiko,' he said.

Umiko circled the whole room before she finally got to him.

'They're having a wonderful time out there,' she said, looking through the gap, out over the party in the

street. 'It's the feeling from the sorrow creatures. You see, I can help grownups too!'

'Look closer,' said Dr M.

Then Umiko noticed the children; how they were standing apart from one another, neither happy nor sad, just blank. She turned and looked over at Morcambe, who stood in a corner looking very similar.

'But that isn't what happened to me,' she said quietly. 'I haven't gone all blank and useless like that . . . I'm very useful . . .'

'Perhaps that is because you still have some sorrows left inside,' said Dr M.

Julian Wells clinked glasses with Constable Hocroft. He felt fantastic. It was a lovely evening for a street party, and although his old home town often made him feel a little sad, it was really great to be here. In the magically happy atmosphere of Zoffany Strand he was sure they'd sort this business of his missing Stanley soon enough. Nothing to worry about at all. Constable

Hocroft was a good policeman; he'd
even come to meet Julian at the train
station. Julian swigged his drink and
batted a balloon. The balloon (white,
with a Dracula smile drawn on in
marker-pen) bounced gently off a little
girl's head and floated up, trailing its
ribbon. The girl didn't even look at the
balloon; she just carried on humming
to herself.

That tune . . . everyone's into that tune these days, thought Julian as he watched the balloon bob past. It risked popping on Constable Hocroft's hat and lined up the Dracula smile with two eerie puffball eyes.

Julian's glass smashed beside him as he fell down fast asleep on the pavement.

'Umm, Doctor? You should maybe look outside again,' said Stanley, peering out through the window gap down onto Zoffany Strand, which was now scattered with sleeping adult bodies and unconcerned, humming children.

No answer.

The first thing that Stanley saw when he turned round wasn't Dr M

– he couldn't spot him anywhere; what he saw were three wenlocks, each one larger and more looming than he'd seen before. Umiko was stretched out on the floor, asleep, and there was Dr M fast asleep beside her, buried in spotty creatures, his pipe still sticking out of his mouth like a periscope. The whole scene was repeated kaleidoscopically on either side by the mirrors.

Stanley turned back to the window again to avoid the wenlocks' sleepy gaze. His ears were filled with the *thud-thud-thud* of his own heartbeat and his stomach had turned upside down. He was terrified. Without thinking about what he was doing, he began to undo the clasps on his instrument case. He turned it over a couple of times – there was always one silly clasp that he forgot.

'A remarkably sturdy boy' – that's what Dr M had called him earlier. He didn't feel sturdy now, not a bit, but he was the only one who could help now. He must try to stay awake. His fingers shook like cornered mice.

He had not slept on the train. He had mistaken the wenlock for a ticket inspector and maybe that was why. Perhaps he could be mistaken again, this time deliberately.

First he imagined the wenlocks behind him into a variety of comedy hats. A red fez, like performing monkeys wear, one of those cork-dangling Australian ones, and a knight's shiny helmet. This was distracting enough to get his ukulele into his hands. Then Stanley dressed them in stripy, dotty, flowery-bright circus patterns and began to play, still facing the window.

He still couldn't quite get it, that tune that the no-longer-worried children hummed. Then for a moment he found a bit of it and his humble little four-stringed instrument suddenly sounded quite different to its usual self. For a second it sounded as though it had many more strings than four. The noise rose all around him like a choir, but then Stanley's playing faltered and the strings immediately sounded like their own lonely selves again.

Once more he turned back to face into the room and found himself staring into a wall of cream-coloured cloth. Not stripy, silly or circus coloured, just towering wenlock cloth. They were standing right over him with that terrible stillness he'd seen before on the one by the canal. He felt woozy and tired, and stumbled back a step. Then suddenly Stanley had it; he had the tune in his mind as though he'd sieved the whole thing from a pan of sand. He played it there and then.

The wenlocks lost their stillness. They flickered and whooshed about, reflected everywhere at once, and below them the sorrow creatures sang with Stanley. They had little owlish, round voices to go with their roundish shapes, so calm and perfect, but together as loud as a choir. This was a tune that they all knew. Stanley had not noticed what a pretty one it was before. It was caught up in his mind with the blank style of humming from the non-worried children on the canal and at the street party, but here, with this lovely, ridiculous choir, it was so light, and yet serious, like a dance in a cemetery.

Now the wenlocks dipped and bobbed over the sorrow creatures, as though they were trying to dampen the chorus with their cloth, but the little singers flowed out of their way like so many rubber ducks on a choppy pond. From the centre of this pond a certain creature, which Stanley recognized as the extra lumpy one he'd been looking for amongst the crowd, rose speedily into the air to hang, up-rumped, at about the height of a person. The chorus went on, but this creature seemed to hold its breath. Morcambe's sorrow creature began to swell like a balloon, inflated by the music.

At a point where the music changed direction, the inflated creature suddenly popped like a small firework and dusted the already dusty air with a little cloud. There, in the rolling, jellyfish vapour was poor Morcambe, endlessly running from the swarm of grey-blue cats that were trying to steal his tail.

In a corner of the room, the real Morcambe sat up and sniffed the air. Brightness returned to his eyes and his fur bristled in waves. His cloud drifted determinedly across to him and he simply breathed the whole thing in with a quick hiss.

Morcambe shivered, sneezed once, and then a grin slid across his face and he was himself again. There were frights in that cloud, but they were his very own. Standing on all fours, he shook his behind and made threatening lunges towards the wenlocks. All three of them were suddenly towering over him and he growled at them from behind his toothy smile. One of the three flinched away more than the others: this one obviously remembered Morcambe and his teeth from the train.

Then Morcambe truly got his energy up, and within a furry, blurry second all three wenlocks were looking down at long gashes and tears in their cloth. Within another moment they weren't wenlocks at all any more.

Their shredded cloth slipped to the floor, their pom-pom eyes rolled into dusty corners, and all that was left

around Morcambe were three heaping, teetering piles of sorrow creatures.

Stanley stopped playing, put down his ukulele and started to clap. The room fell silent, save for a pair of differently pitched snores coming from Dr M and Umiko, still out cold on the floor, and Stanley's quickly fading applause. Morcambe looked over at Stanley, wagged his whole self furiously, and was suddenly buried as the three great piles of creatures collapsed and spread out over the room. The creatures rolled out and out until the floor was several sorrows deep all over. In the mirrors on either side they stretched out for miles and miles and miles.

With a rustling sound and a muffled cough, a small, black-sleeved hand holding a pipe emerged from the deep-layered carpet of spotty beasts. Another hand emerged to light the pipe. Then the whole of Dr M, including some very crumpled ears, stood up and looked thoughtfully around the room. After a moment he waded, thigh-deep, across to Stanley.

'The wenlocks are gone?' he asked.

'This is what's left of them,' said Stanley, nodding at the many, many sorrow creatures.

'A poor man's feast,' said Dr M dryly. 'There's more at the end than at the beginning. How on earth . . . ?'

'I remembered the tune.'

Dr M looked perplexed. Stanley fished about amongst the creatures and pulled out his ukulele.

'This one,' he said, and played a stretch of the music. The room roared immediately with the sorrow choir and another creature shot into the air, expanded and popped into a picture-cloud (a child's bed with a dark, dark gap beneath, where crocodile teeth glinted). Dr M drew in his chin and shook his head, wide eyed. The cloud sped to the window and squeezed its way out through the small gap.

'Well, well. For goodness' sake don't stop. You might forget it again!' said Dr M.

'What happened?' said Umiko blearily. She swept up an armful of creatures and let them fall again like gold pieces in a pirate's treasure cave.

'Show her, Stanley,' said Dr M.

Stanley played. Dr M knotted his ears; this choir was loud! Sorrows began to rise and burst with the rhythm. The sorrow-clouds gathered at the boarded windows, clumped and eager to return to the children outside.

'Umiko, help me with these boards,' shouted Dr M. He was pulling at the window board where a large cloud (inside which a small city was burning to the ground) tried to squash through the gap. Umiko crossed the room slowly. Her head tilted back as she watched the gathering clouds above, each one brimming with a small, sad, terrible story, or

a worry of some sort or another: parents replaced by robots, missing guinea-pigs, tall-hatted witches, slurpy quicksand. Frights too strange to explain: a four-poster bed all covered with growing grass; looming and ominous giraffes with mean, arching eyebrows; doors that led out of impossibly high walls; taps that dripped in secret, shadowy places. In some there were cruel-looking people: mean faces, laughing boys and girls with pointing fingers. Others showed people just doing everyday things: reading a book, or riding a bicycle; getting into a car, or carrying a tray of drinks. In many of these quieter clouds, which were like little pieces of the past, the mind's image of someone who has only just left the room, was a woman with dark hair and shining, nervous eyes. Here she danced (terribly); there she sat hunched with a needle and thread. And in lots and lots and lots she played with a little dark-haired girl.

Umiko reached the window and pulled down the piece of board that Dr M had only managed to loosen. The room was flooded with light for an instant but was darkened again as the inside clouds rushed for freedom. Stanley kept playing, the sorrows kept singing, rising and popping, but already they grew quieter because more than half of them had burst.

Morcambe bounced about the emptying floor, snapping up at the sorrows as they hung, ready to pop. Dr Moon looked on, puffing his pipe with an air of satisfaction. Umiko sat and

watched the clouds slipping out of the window above her one by one. Many seemed keen to escape, but they were jostling and folding over one another too, and some were hanging back.

Then at last Stanley found that his music was down to his own lonely four strings. A sorrow hung silently in the air and then, *phwip!* it burst into one last scene: Aya Lee and her daughter, with broad smiles, folding a monster from a sheet of paper.

Umiko Lee sighed deeply and looked up at the clouds above, where they hung at person height like a forest mist. There were none left that

wanted to leave by the open window; they shimmered in its light. Then she breathed them all in, like Morcambe had done with his; the whole lot, in one small breath. Umiko sighed again, then hiccupped.

The sun was glowing low in the evening sky as Stanley Wells, Dr Moon, Morcambe and Umiko Lee stood at the glassless window of the Eva Lückes School for Dance and Special Movement. In the street below, tables and chairs, bottles and balloons were silently being tidied away. Here and there people sat or stood, quietly puzzled. But bumping and scampering around the party-tidying, head-scratching grown-ups were children of all shapes and sizes. They laughed and screeched, sleeve-pulled, whinged and wriggled as though Zoffany Strand was a home-time playground. From up in the window you could hear their voices:

'I've got a crocodile under my bed that could chomp you whole.'

'I've got a tap in my cupboard that could wash you into next week.'

'I don't like
seaweed at all.'

'She filled my school bag
with chalk-dust.'

'Come and visit! There are
slugs in our garden that will
eat you up if you go down
the slide the wrong way.'

'He's got nasty elbows, but
I pushed him in the nose.'

'My dad says his
over-giraffe will eat
him one day.'

'I'm so tired, my
hair has gone
all warm.'

162

'Excuse me, have you seen a little boy in a green jacket? He's usually got a little instrument case with him.'

'Dad!' shouted Stanley, waving his ukulele box out of the window. 'I'll be right down!'

He looked at Umiko. She was petting Morcambe quietly.

'Your dad still has one creature – what will you do with it? I don't think it will have heard the music,' said Stanley.

'Oh . . . I don't know,' said Umiko. 'I remember that tune though' – she hummed a snatch – 'but maybe me and Dad will need that one beast for a bit longer.'

'We'll take an evening boat ride,' said Dr Moon. 'Albert should be finished tidying the boat for you by the

time we get there.'

'You haven't made him tidy the boat! Oh, my poor pa! Our boat was never meant to be tidy; it just isn't cut out for it,' said Umiko with a half-smile.

Dr E. B. Moon shook Stanley by the hand. 'Good job, Stanley,' he said. 'Sturdy work. We'll surely be in touch.'

Morcambe grinned and wagged his whole body; Dr M tipped his hat for him. Stanley scratched Morcambe lightly on the nose and ran for the door. As he took the stairs three at a time he wondered how Dr M would find him again. Surely he wouldn't have too much trouble.

'What in the world have you been up to?' said Julian, lifting Stanley in his arms.

'It's a sad story, Dad. But you'll never believe it,' said Stanley.

'Well, come on now, we can just make the last train. You've some explaining to do on the way. And I'll have to explain to Constable Hocroft later.'

'I think I'm getting quite good with this thing,' said Stanley Wells, waggling his instrument case.

'I think I lost a whole afternoon somewhere,' said Julian Wells.

These are the chords that
Stanley knows for his ukelele.

(Tuning *G C E A*)

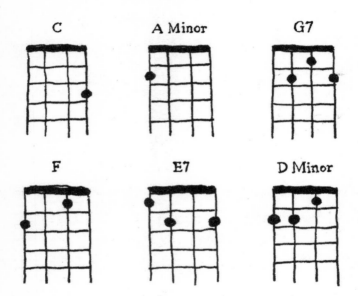

C   A Minor   G7

F   E7   D Minor

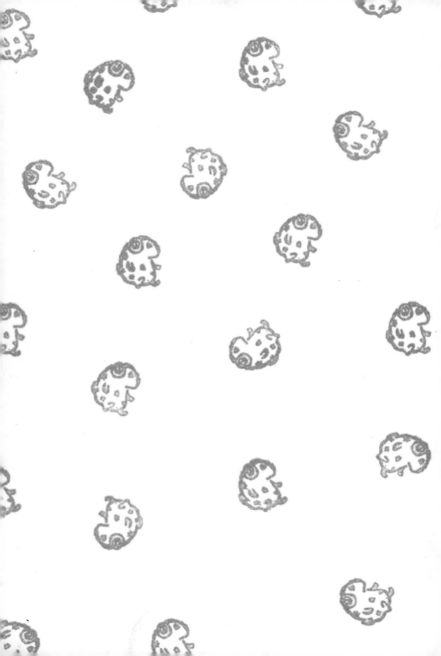